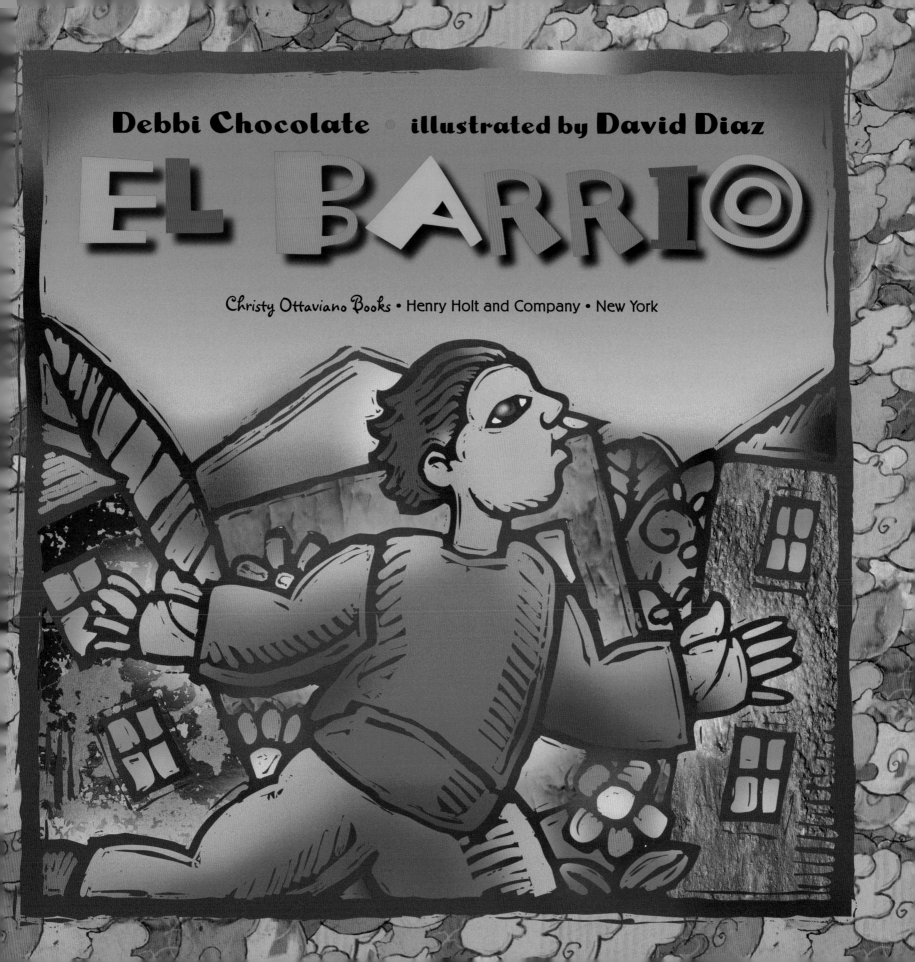

Debbi Chocolate ® illustrated by **David Diaz**

EL BARRIO

Christy Ottaviano Books • Henry Holt and Company • New York

This is *el barrio*!
My home in the city
with its rain-washed murals
and sparkling graffiti.

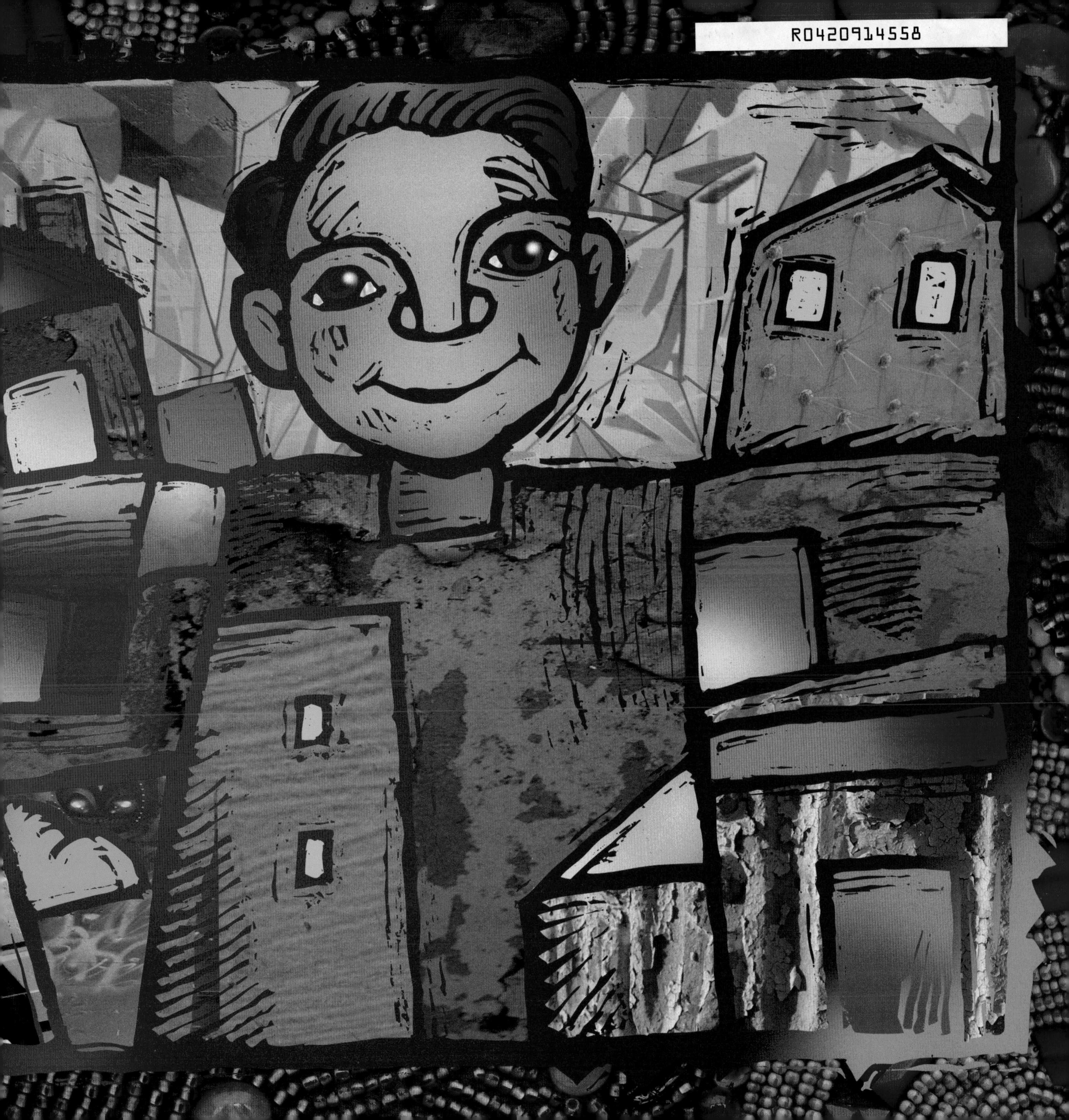

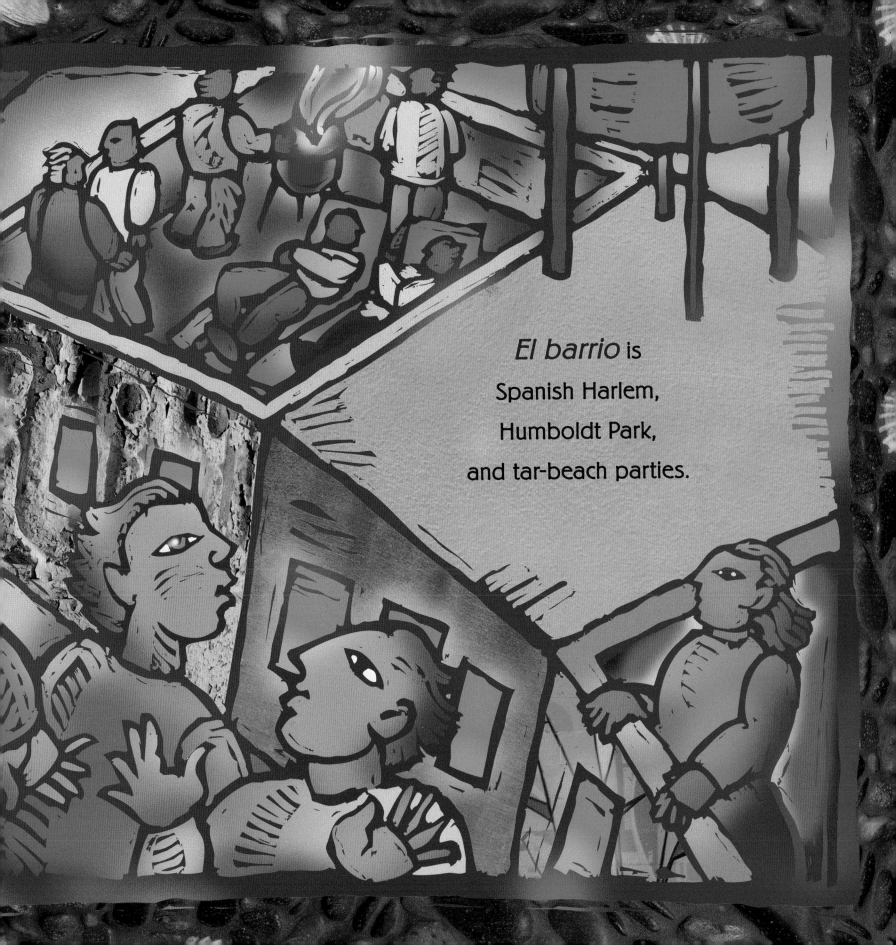

El barrio is
Spanish Harlem,
Humboldt Park,
and tar-beach parties.

El barrio is where Nativity parades,

Cinco de Mayo,

and Day of the Dead

explode into big holidays.

Feliz Navidad!

El barrio is a *quinceañera* party
(my sister turns fifteen today!)
and a swollen birthday *piñata*
bursting with candy treasure.

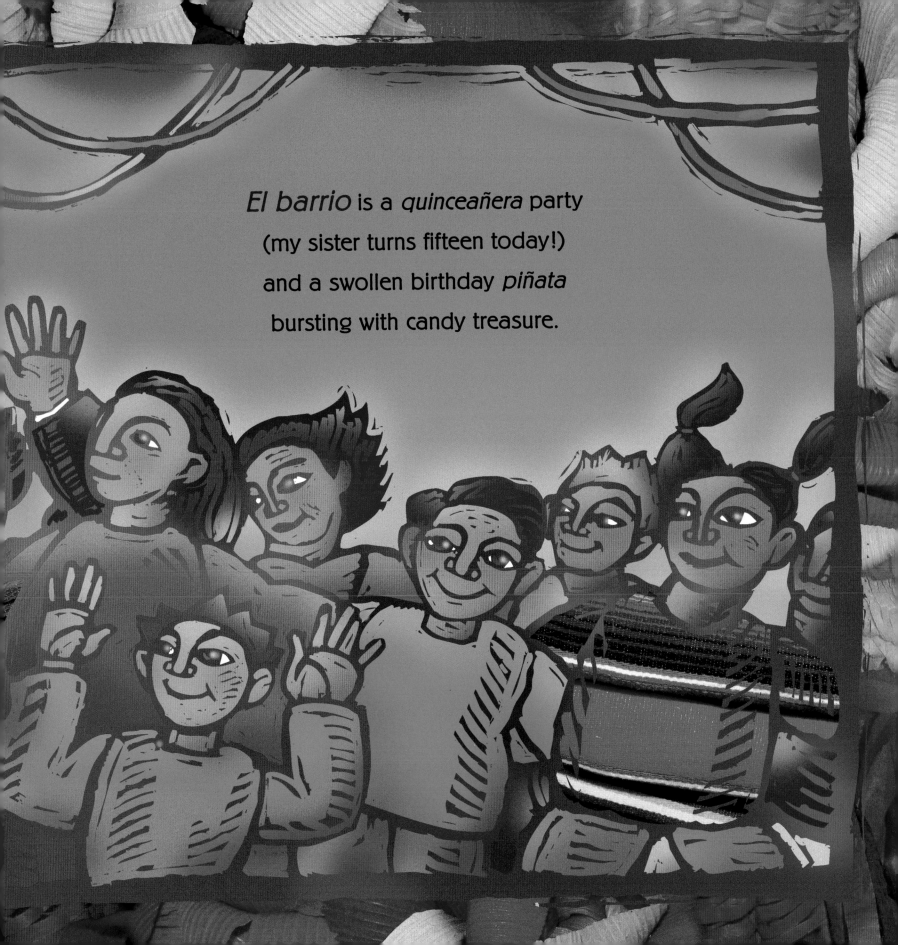

El barrio is where my cousins come

from lots of different lands—

Mexico, Colombia, Puerto Rico, and Cuba—

and where on Sundays

Aztec eyes and Mayan faces

go to *la iglesia* to pray.

This is a picture of my sister

at her First Communion.

El barrio is silver-streaked tenements,
neon city streets,
storefront churches,
and *bodegas* that never sleep.

El barrio is where, sometimes at night,

Grandfather plays a soft *bolero* on his guitar.

He sings to me and my sister of the olden days.

This *rosario* once belonged to my grandmother.

Now it belongs to my sister.

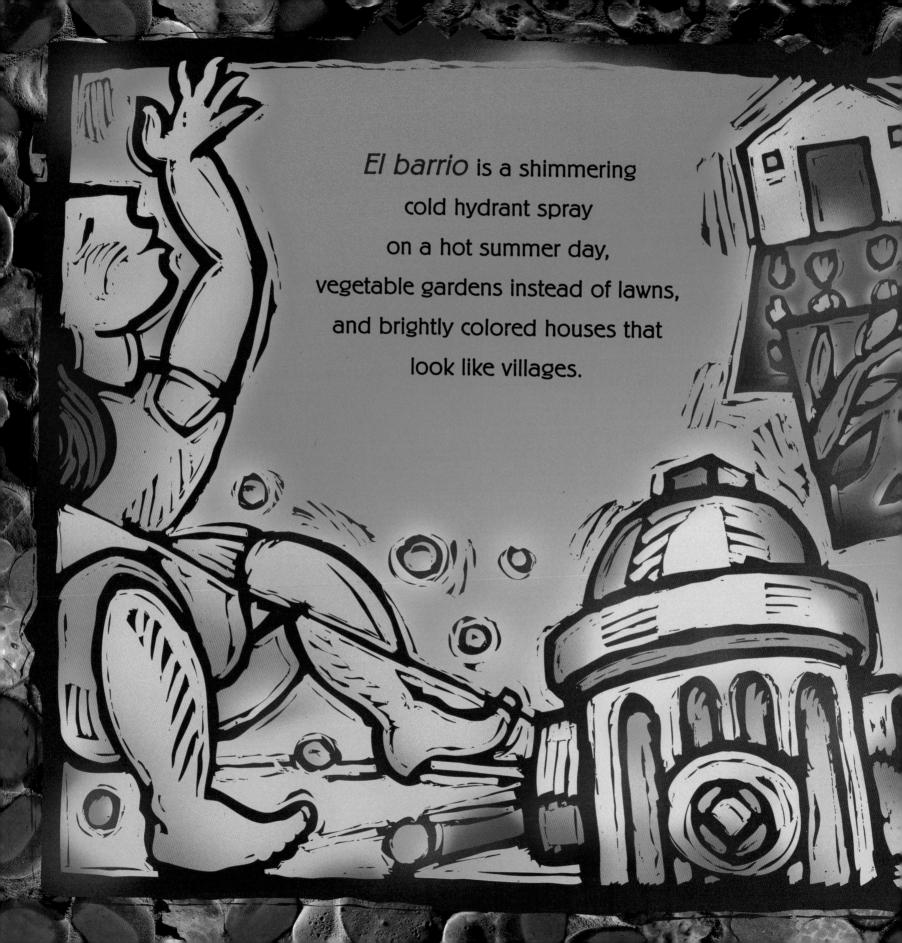

El barrio is a shimmering
cold hydrant spray
on a hot summer day,
vegetable gardens instead of lawns,
and brightly colored houses that
look like villages.

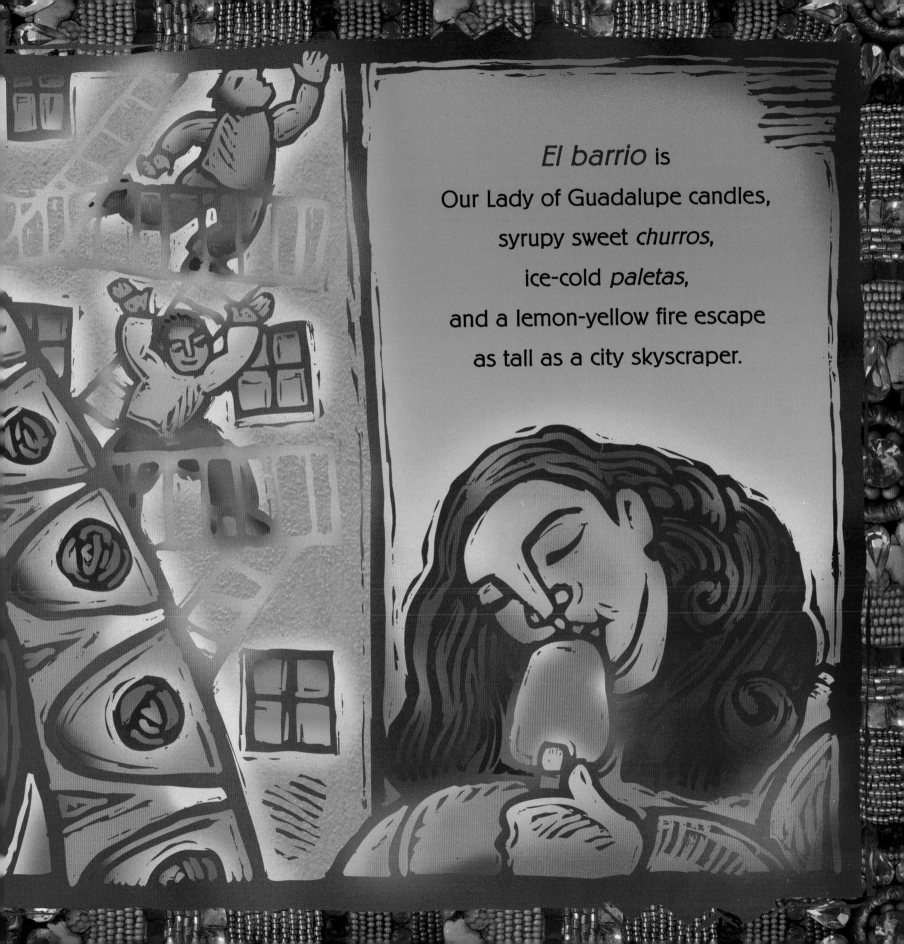

El barrio is
Our Lady of Guadalupe candles,
syrupy sweet *churros*,
ice-cold *paletas*,
and a lemon-yellow fire escape
as tall as a city skyscraper.

El barrio is a *quinceañera* mass,
a chiffon dress,
a bouquet of roses
for Our Lady of Guadalupe's brown hands.
Papi places a glittering *corona* on my sister's head.

El barrio is a heartbeat.
Shhh, listen!
It's the sound of blaring trumpets,
tejano, and *salsa* music
tickling my feet!
The *mariachis* play at all the *quinceañeras*
in my neighborhood.

El barrio is a *quinceañera* waltz,
my sister gliding across the floor with *Papi*
whose heart is filled with pride and love.
Today, my beautiful sister looks all grown up.

El barrio is where my grandparents,
dancing to a slow *ranchera* at dusk,
bring the crowd to their feet.

On this special day,
my sister gives her baby dolls away
to the little girls at her *quinceañera*.

El barrio is where
my sister whispers in my ear,
"You made my *quinceañera* special
just by being here."

This is *el barrio*!

My home in the city.

GLOSSARY

barrio (BAHR-ree-oh).   Neighborhood.

bodega (bo-DAY-gah).   Grocery store.

bolero (boh-LEHR-roh).   Traditional Mexican song or music.

churros (CHEWR-rohs).   Sticks of crispy fried dough coated in sugar with a cakey center.

Cinco de Mayo (SEEN-coh day MY-oh). May 5 celebration of Mexican heritage and pride.

corona (core-ROH-nah).   A crown.

Feliz Navidad (fay-LEESE nah-vee-DAHD). Merry Christmas.

Humboldt Park.   A predominately Latino neighborhood in Chicago.

iglesia (ee-GLAY-see-ah).   A church.

mariachis (mar-ree-AH-chees).   Musicians who dress and play in a style typical of Mexico.

Our Lady of Guadalupe (gwa-dah-LOO-pay). Mary, the mother of Jesus and patron saint of Mexico.

paletas (pah-LAY-tahs).   Popsicles.

piñata (peen-YAH-tah).   Large, brightly colored paper toy filled with candy and/or small toys.

papi (POP-pee).   Papa.

quinceañera (KEEN-say-ahn-YAY-rah). A Latina girl's fifteenth birthday.

ranchera (rahn-CHAIR-rah).   Traditional Mexican song or music.

rosario (roh-SAR-ree-oh).   Rosary.

salsa (SAHL-sah).   Spanish Caribbean music popular across Latin America.

Spanish Harlem.   A predominately Latino neighborhood in New York City.

tejano (tay-HAH-noh).   Folk and popular music originating from Hispanic Texans of Central and South Texas.

Para mi hermanita, Nina Williams—
con amor
—D. C.

For Denise
—D. D.

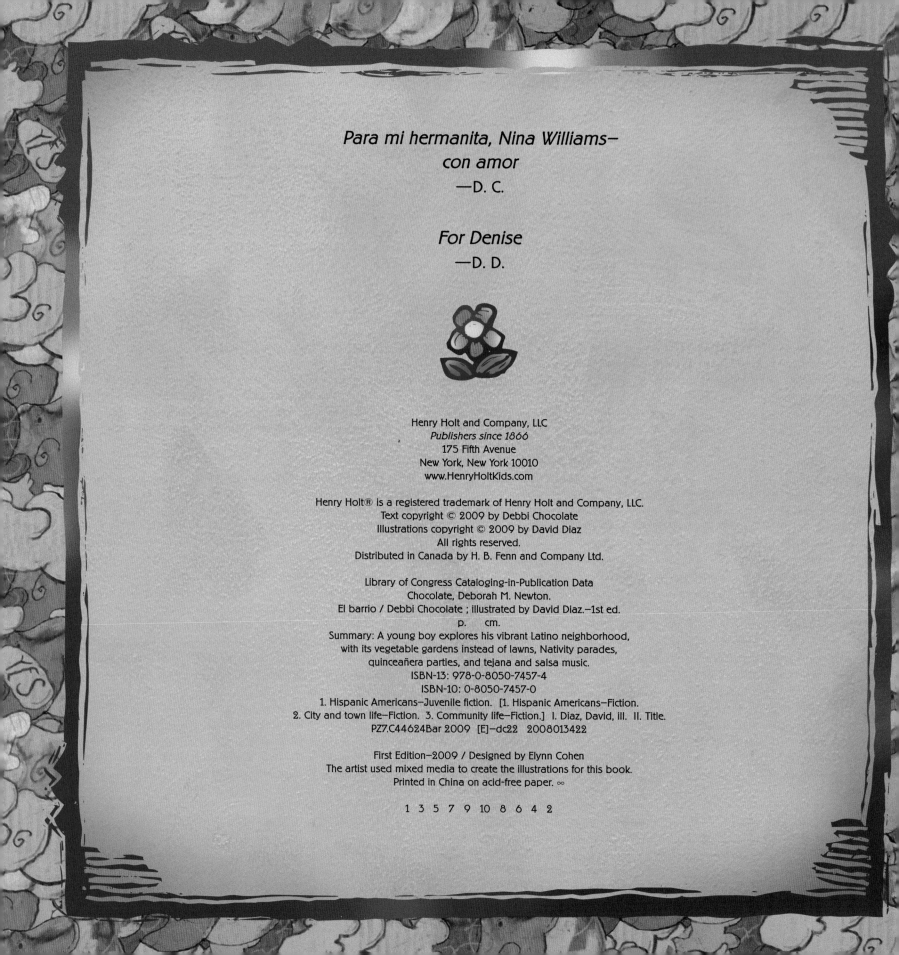

Henry Holt and Company, LLC
Publishers since 1866
175 Fifth Avenue
New York, New York 10010
www.HenryHoltKids.com

Library of Congress Cataloging-in-Publication Data
Chocolate, Deborah M. Newton.
El barrio / Debbi Chocolate ; illustrated by David Diaz.—1st ed.
p.   cm.
Summary: A young boy explores his vibrant Latino neighborhood,
with its vegetable gardens instead of lawns, Nativity parades,
quinceañera parties, and tejana and salsa music.
ISBN-13: 978-0-8050-7457-4
ISBN-10: 0-8050-7457-0
1. Hispanic Americans—Juvenile fiction. [1. Hispanic Americans—Fiction.
2. City and town life—Fiction. 3. Community life—Fiction.] I. Diaz, David, ill. II. Title.
PZ7.C44624Bar 2009 [E]—dc22 2008013422

First Edition—2009 / Designed by Elynn Cohen
The artist used mixed media to create the illustrations for this book.
Printed in China on acid-free paper. ∞

1 3 5 7 9 10 8 6 4 2